A Note to Parents and Caregivers:

Read-it! Readers are for children who are just starting on the amazing road to reading. These beautiful books support both the acquisition of reading skills and the love of books.

The RED LEVEL presents familiar topics using common words and repeating sentence patterns.
The BLUE LEVEL presents new ideas using a larger vocabulary and varied sentence structure.
The YELLOW LEVEL presents more challenging ideas, a broad vocabulary, and wide variety in sentence structure.

When sharing a book with your child, read in short stretches, pausing often to talk about the pictures. Have your child turn the pages and point to the pictures and familiar words. And be sure to reread favorite stories or parts of stories.

There is no right or wrong way to share books with children. Find time to read with your child, and pass on the legacy of literacy.

Adria F. Klein, Ph.D.
Professor Emeritus
California State University
San Bernardino, California

First American edition published in 2003 by
Picture Window Books
5115 Excelsior Boulevard
Suite 232
Minneapolis, MN 55416
1-877-845-8392
www.picturewindowbooks.com

First published in Great Britain by Franklin Watts, 96 Leonard Street, London, EC2A 4XD
Text © Andy Blackford 2000
Illustration © Tim Archbold 2000

Printed in the United States of America.

Library of Congress Cataloging-in-Publication Data
Blackford, Andy.
  Little Joe's big race / written by Andy Blackford ; illustrated by Tim Archbold.—1st
American ed.
    p. cm. — (Read-it! readers)
  Summary: After Little Joe wins the egg and spoon race on Sports Day, he gets so excited
that he continues to carry the egg and then its hatched chicken for another year.
  ISBN 1-4048-0063-8
  [1. Racing—Fiction. 2. Eggs—Fiction. 3. Chickens—Fiction.] I. Archbold, Tim, ill. II. Title. III.
Series.
  PZ7.B53228 Li 2003
  [E]—dc21   2002074930

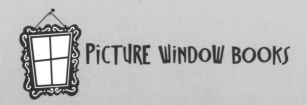

PICTURE WINDOW BOOKS

Little Joe's Big Race

Written by Andy Blackford

Illustrated by Tim Archbold

Reading Advisors:
Adria F. Klein, Ph.D.
Professor Emeritus, California State University
San Bernardino, California

Ruth Thomas
Durham Public Schools
Durham, North Carolina

R. Ernice Bookout
Durham Public Schools
Durham, North Carolina

Picture Window Books
Minneapolis, Minnesota

Little Joe didn't like
Field Day.

He was so little, a frog
could jump higher.

He was so slow, a turtle
could run faster.

But Little Joe was good at balancing things.

He decided to win
the egg-and-spoon race.

And Little Joe did win!

But he was so excited,
he forgot to stop.

He ran out of the school yard

and through the town.

He ran all day

and all night, too.

He swam through rivers.

He ran up

and down mountains.

One day, there was a loud CRACK!

Out of the egg popped
a chicken.

Still Joe kept running.

He ran through the sun

and through the rain.

Soon, the chicken grew
too big for the spoon.

Little Joe had to carry him on a shovel.

At the same time,
Little Joe grew bigger
and bigger.

One year later, Little Joe arrived back at school.

It was Field Day again.
Everyone was cheering.

"Good job, Big Joe!"
cried the teacher.

"You've won the chicken-
and-shovel race!"

And she gave Joe and
the chicken a medal.

Red Level

The Best Snowman, by Margaret Nash 1-4048-0048-4
Bill's Baggy Pants, by Susan Gates 1-4048-0050-6
Cleo and Leo, by Anne Cassidy 1-4048-0049-2
Felix on the Move, by Maeve Friel 1-4048-0055-7
Jasper and Jess, by Anne Cassidy 1-4048-0061-1
The Lazy Scarecrow, by Jillian Powell 1-4048-0062-X
Little Joe's Big Race, by Andy Blackford 1-4048-0063-8
The Little Star, by Deborah Nash 1-4048-0065-4
The Naughty Puppy, by Jillian Powell 1-4048-0067-0
Selfish Sophie, by Damian Kelleher 1-4048-0069-7

Blue Level

The Bossy Rooster, by Margaret Nash 1-4048-0051-4
Jack's Party, by Ann Bryant 1-4048-0060-3
Little Red Riding Hood, by Maggie Moore 1-4048-0064-6
Recycled!, by Jillian Powell 1-4048-0068-9
The Sassy Monkey, by Anne Cassidy 1-4048-0058-1
The Three Little Pigs, by Maggie Moore 1-4048-0071-9

Yellow Level

Cinderella, by Barrie Wade 1-4048-0052-2
The Crying Princess, by Anne Cassidy 1-4048-0053-0
Eight Enormous Elephants, by Penny Dolan 1-4048-0054-9
Freddie's Fears, by Hilary Robinson 1-4048-0056-5
Goldilocks and the Three Bears, by Barrie Wade 1-4048-0057-3
Mary and the Fairy, by Penny Dolan 1-4048-0066-2
Jack and the Beanstalk, by Maggie Moore 1-4048-0059-X
The Three Billy Goats Gruff, by Barrie Wade 1-4048-0070-0